DON'T WORRY, BE HAPPY

LEARNING ABOUT SEPARATION ANXIETY

Katherine Eason

FOX EYE
PUBLISHING

Layla was a big girl now. It was nearly her **FIRST DAY AT SCHOOL**. Mum took Layla to see the school. It seemed very large to Layla.

Layla woke up in the night. She had a **BAD DREAM**. She dreamed that Mum didn't fetch her from school. Layla felt **WORRIED**. What if her dream came true?

The next day, Gran came to look after Layla while Mum went out. Layla didn't want Mum to go. What if something happened, and Mum didn't come back? Layla felt **WORRIED**.

Mum took Layla shopping for new clothes for school. Layla cried. She trembled. She said she didn't want to go to school.

Mum helped Layla to take big, slow breaths. They pretended to blow up a big, red balloon. Layla **CALMED DOWN**.

They talked about Layla's **WORRY HEAD**. They called it Wilbur Worry! Mum said Wilbur Worry keeps you safe, but sometimes he shouts a little too loudly.

Mum and Layla made a **WORRY BOX**. Layla drew her **WORRIES**. She drew herself lost and alone at school. She drew Mum waving goodbye. She put the pictures in the box.

Mum and Layla looked at the pictures.

Mum said it was OK to feel worried. She said Layla could always talk to her about her worries. But Mum knew Layla was very brave. She knew she would be OK.

She asked Layla what she would do if she felt **WORRIED** at school. Layla thought about it.

On the first day of school, Wilbur Worry started shouting. Layla told him to be quiet. She told him she was safe. Layla pretended to blow up a big, red balloon. She thought about her favourite things. She **CALMED DOWN**.

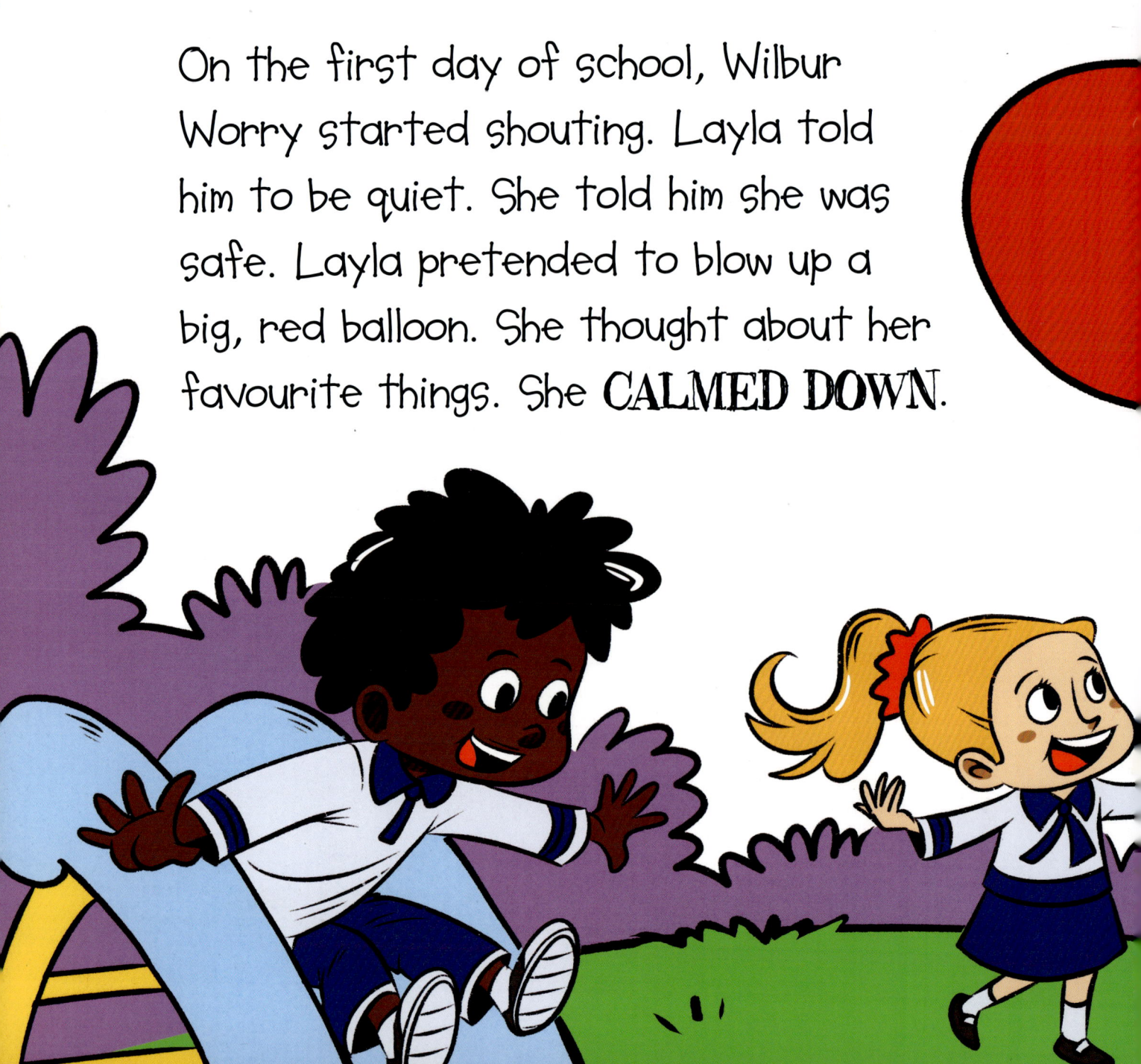

Layla had a wonderful day! She had learnt to **MANAGE HER WORRIES**.

Words and Behaviour

Layla didn't know how to manage her worries in this story and that caused a lot of problems.

WORRIED

WORRIES

WORRY HEAD

Let's talk about emotions and behaviour

This series helps children to understand difficult emotions and behaviours and how to manage them. The characters in the series have been created to show emotions and behaviours that are often seen in young children, and which can be difficult to manage.

Don't Worry, Be Happy!

The story in this book examines the reasons for managing your worries. It looks at why calming down is important and how managing your worries helps people to overcome their fears.

How to use this book

You can read this book with one child or a group of children. The book can be used to begin a discussion around complex behaviour such as managing separation anxiety.

The book is also a reading aid, with enlarged and repeated words to help children to develop their reading skills.

How to read the story

Before beginning the story, ensure that the children you are reading to are relaxed and focused.

Take time to look at the enlarged words and the illustrations, and discuss what this book might be about before reading the story.

New words can be tricky for young children to approach. Sounding them out first, slowly and repeatedly, can help children to learn the words and become familiar with them.

How to discuss the story

When you have finished reading the story, use these questions and discussion points to examine the theme of the story with children and explore the emotions and behaviour within it:
- What do you think the story was about?
- Have you been in a situation in which you felt worried? What was that situation?
- Do you think managing your worries doesn't matter? Why?
- Do you think managing your worries is important? Why?
- What could go wrong if you don't manage your worries?

Titles in the series

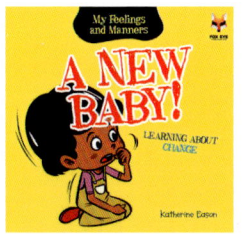 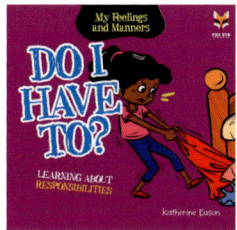  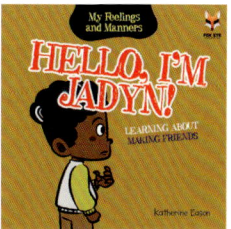 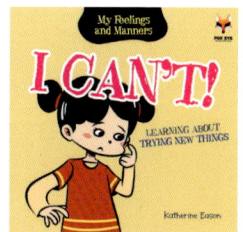

 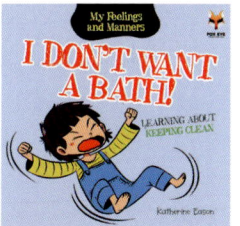 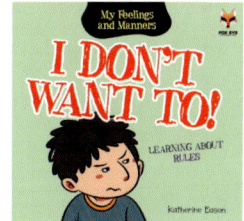 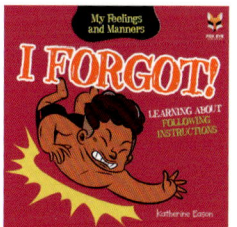 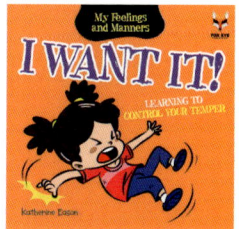

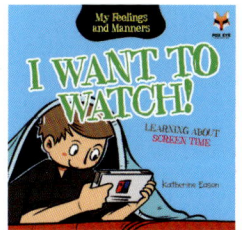  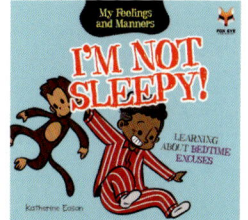 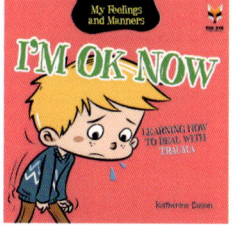 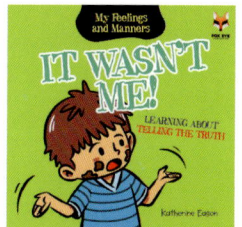

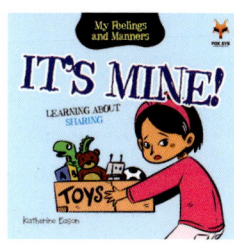  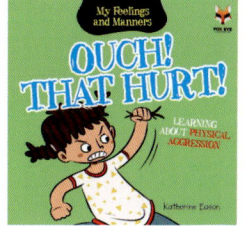 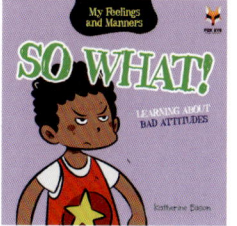 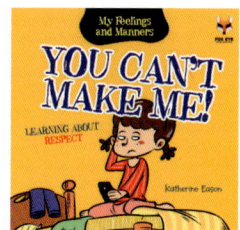

First published in 2023 by Fox Eye Publishing
Unit 31, Vulcan House Business Centre,
Vulcan Road, Leicester, LE5 3EF
www.foxeyepublishing.com

Copyright © 2023 Fox Eye Publishing
All rights reserved. No portion of this book may be reproduced in any form without permission from the publisher, except as permitted by U.K. copyright law.

Author: Katherine Eason
Art director: Paul Phillips
Cover designer: Emily Bailey
Editor: Jenny Rush

All illustrations by Novel

ISBN 978-1-80445-175-5

Printed in China